The Friendly Monster

MYRIAD BOOKS LIMITED
35 Bishopsthorpe Road, London SE26 4PA

First published in Belgium and the Netherlands in 2006 by Clavis Uitgeverij,
Hasselt-Amsterdam..

Text and illustrations copyright © 2006 Clavis Uitgeverij, Hasselt-Amsterdam.
All rights reserved.
www.clavisbooks.com

ISBN 1 84746 065 8
EAN 978 184746 065 3

Printed in China

www.myriadbooks.com

The Friendly Monster

Guy Didelez | Ruby Kersten

MYRIAD BOOKS LIMITED

George is watching a cartoon about monsters. It seems so real that monsters could crawl out of the television set any moment. George forgets his Mummy and Daddy are there. He can only see those crooked, super scary monsters. Bump, bump, bump goes his heartbeat. Imagine if a monster came to my room later this evening...

"You have to stay in your bed," Daddy says. George stares at his father with a frightened look in his eyes. "But what if a monster appears?" Daddy laughs. "Just dream about a funny monster. I am sure you will become best friends."

George huddles deeply under his sheets. That's the only place where he is safe from the monsters. But... what is that noise? A rustling underneath his bed! Is it a monster? George feels his mattress rising up. Very carefully he peeps from underneath his sheets.

"Ha haa! Here I am!" A round and furry monster appears from underneath his bed.
But this monster is not at all like those scary ones on television. He's very funny, with a bump on top of his head. And he smiles at George. George knows at once that this is a Friendly Monster.

"I am here for you! Only you can see me. And I can do magic. Look!" shouts the monster. There are lights twinkling everywhere. There are flags and lanterns as well. The Friendly Monster takes George by the hand and whirls him around the room.

The Friendly Monster is standing on his head. "Can you do this?" he asks. How wonderful the world looks upside down! George and the Friendly Monster giggle so hard that they fall on the floor. Then they start folding paper aeroplanes. Look how they fly! "Let's go downstairs!" says Monster, "I'm thirsty." But George remembers that Daddy told him to stay in his room.

Too late! The Friendly Monster has already reached the stairs. George follows very carefully, hoping Mummy and Daddy are already sleeping. The Friendly Monster is so big that the stairs make a loud creaking noise.

When they open the fridge, George and the Friendly Monster get very excited. "Orange juice, ice cream, cakes and bananas," shouts the Friendly Monster. George and the Monster eat as much as they want. "If you eat sweet things, you have to brush your teeth," says the Monster. "Let's go to the bathroom!"

George and the Friendly Monster make silly faces in front of the mirror. The Monster pulls one of George's socks over the bump on his head like a nightcap. But... what's that noise? They can hear footsteps! It's Daddy! Will he get angry at George for not staying in his bed?

"What are you doing here?" Daddy asks.
"Cl... clea... cleaning my teeth ..." George says.
"But I thought you were afraid of monsters?" He smiles at George and doesn't even see the Friendly Monster sticking a finger in each of his ears! George is the only one who can hear, see and feel the Monster!

Back in his room, George curls up in the Friendly Monster's warm arms. "Read to me," he asks the Monster, "please!" Soon the reading makes George so tired that his eyes nearly close. "You are tired", says the Friendly Monster. "We'll have a look at the stars for just one moment and then I'll tuck you in."

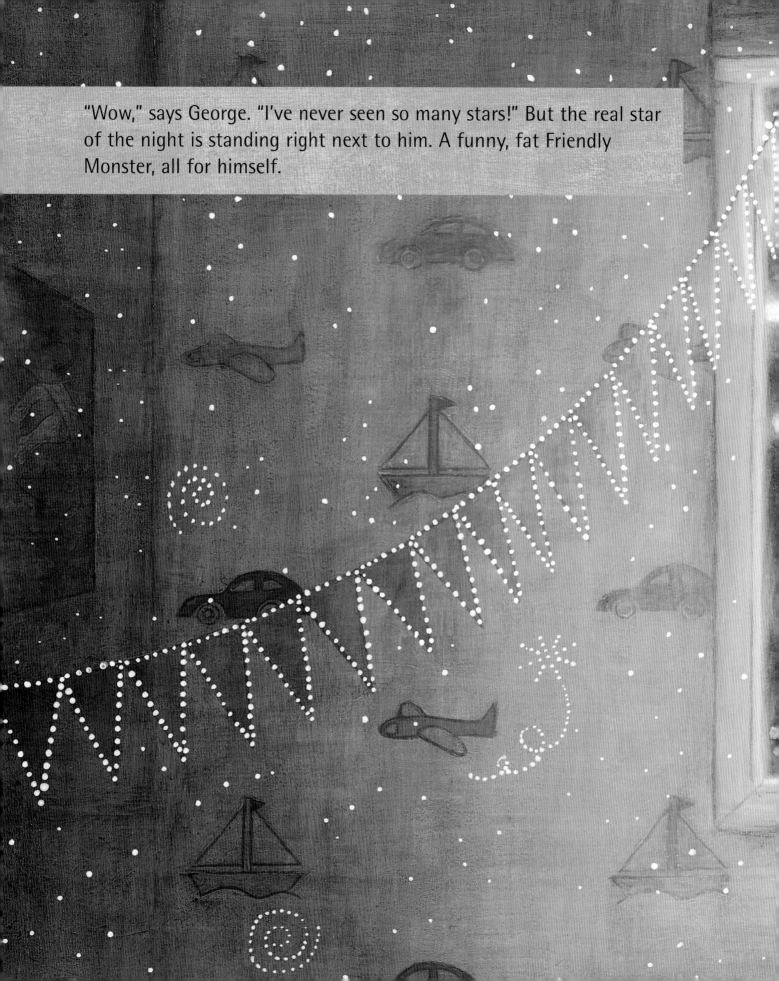

"Wow," says George. "I've never seen so many stars!" But the real star of the night is standing right next to him. A funny, fat Friendly Monster, all for himself.